The Bipolar Bear Family

When a Parent Has Bipolar Disorder

Angela Ann Holloway

AuthorHouse™
1663 Liberty Drive, Suite 200
Bloomington, IN 47403
www.authorhouse.com
Phone: 1-800-839-8640

AuthorHouse™ UK Ltd.
500 Avebury Boulevard
Central Milton Keynes, MK9 2BE
www.authorhouse.co.uk
Phone: 08001974150

This book is a work of fiction. People, places, events, and situations are the product of the authors imagination. Any resemblance to actual persons, living or dead, or historical events, is purely coincidental.

First published by AuthorHouse 8/29/2006

ISBN: 1-4259-2952-4 (sc)

Printed in the United States of America
Bloomington, Indiana

This book is printed on acid-free paper.

Illustrations by Joe Lee

Bloomington, IN   Milton Keynes, UK

authorHOUSE

With love, for
Jr., JD, Chance, and Devynn

And love and gratitude for our
Wonderful Counselor

Not so long ago, in an artic village far away, there lived a polar bear family. There was a papa polar bear, a mama polar bear, and a baby polar bear. And they all loved each other very much, but something was not quite right.

In fact, Baby Bear knew something was wrong. He never said a word, but he worried all the time. He worried about his mom.

You see, Mama Bear had a hard time controlling her feelings. And, sometimes, she did things that upset, and even scared Papa and Baby Bear.

Sometimes Mama Bear would not get out of bed. All day long she would lay under the covers and just cry.

But sometimes, she wouldn't sleep at all. She would laugh and play all day . . .

and all night; even when Papa and Baby Bear wanted to be left alone to rest.

One day, Papa, Mama, and Baby Bear went to the beach to watch the penguins play. They were having a wonderful time. Mama Bear even let Baby Bear have an extra ice-cream sandwich with his lunch. "This is the best day ever!" thought Baby Bear.

On the way home, Baby Bear noticed that Mama Bear was really quiet. Baby Bear thought it was strange because Mama Bear had talked and laughed all day long. "Maybe she just ran out of words and got tired." Baby Bear thought to himself.

"Go in and get ready for bed." Mama Bear said when they got home. Baby Bear started to do as he was told, but when they entered the cave, Mama Bear tripped on a toy Baby Bear had left out on the floor.

Mama Bear leapt to her feet and grabbed Baby Bear by the scruff of the neck. She raised her claw above Baby Bear's head, as if she would squash him. Then, she quickly dropped him to his paws, but let out a very scary roar.

"Stop!" Papa Bear said to Mama Bear.

"Go to Bed!" Mama Bear said to Baby Bear.

"I'm a bad cub!" Baby Bear said to himself, and then mama bear started to cry.

Baby Bear cried too. He quietly cried himself to sleep.

A few days later, Mama Bear had an appointment with the doctor. Baby Bear liked this doctor. She was a kind penguin named Penny, and Dr. Penny had wild berry lollipops!

"Mama Bear has Bipolar Disorder," Dr. Penny explained.

"By . . . what?" Baby Bear asked.

"Bipolar Disorder," Dr. Penny repeated. "It means her brain works differently than many other polar bear brains."

Dr. Penny leaned closer to Baby Bear, "You see, Mama Bear's Brain does not control happy and sad feelings the same way your brain does. That is why she gets very happy; and that is why she gets very sad. It is why she sometimes sleeps a lot, and why she sometimes can't sleep at all."

"And it is why I sometimes do things that scare you and Papa Bear," Mama Bear said gently.

"But I am going to give Mama Bear some special medicine to help control her moods, and her sleep, and all the other things," Dr. Penny said with a comforting smile.

That night Baby Bear could not sleep at all. He was glad that Dr. Penny could help Mama Bear, but he was confused about this Bipolar Disorder. He had a lot of questions, and a few worries. Baby Bear decided to write his questions down on paper and take them to Dr. Penny.

"If my parent gets too happy or too sad, or too mad, is it my fault?"
Absolutely not. You cannot make an adult feel or behave in any certain way; even a parent with Bipolar Disorder.

"If I behave better, will my parent get better?"
No. No matter what your parent says or does, you are not responsible for their behavior. Go ahead and be the best kid you can be, but remember, you did not cause Bipolar Disorder, or Bipolar behavior, just like you did not cause the rain or the snow.

"What does my parent need to do to get better?"
Bipolar Disorder does not go away. It is going to be a part of your family from now on. Therefore, your parent needs to take the right medication every day, as instructed by the doctor. You and

your family should also read more about Bipolar Disorder. Many Bipolar parents go see a counselor, someone they can talk to about their feelings and behavior, or they attend a support group for other grownups with Bipolar Disorder.

"Is Bipolar Disorder a disease? Can I catch it?"
Bipolar Disorder is an illness. That means it makes people not feel well. However, it is not caused by a germ, and therefore you cannot catch it.

"How does someone get Bipolar?"
Bipolar Disorder is inherited. That means we get it from our parents, grandparents, or great grandparents, just like we do our height or eye color. However, it is not passed down as easily as most of the other things we get from our parents.

"Does this mean I will get it?"
Maybe, but that is a big maybe. Even if you do, because your parent has been diagnosed and is getting help, you will do well if you do develop Bipolar Disorder.

"Can I prevent it?"

Possibly. Take care of yourself. Talk about your feelings, get plenty of rest, eat right, and DEFINITELY stay away from alcohol, drugs, and cigarettes. Only take medicine when you are supposed to, and see the doctor regularly.

Baby Bear felt better after talking to Dr. Penny.

Things settled down for the Polar Bear family after that. It wasn't always perfect. Papa Bear had to get used to a slightly different, but less grumpy, Mama Bear. Mama Bear still had some small changes in her mood, and had to learn new ways to not get so angry. And, Baby Bear still acted like . . . well like a Baby Bear. However, for the most part, they all lived happily ever after.

Lightning Source UK Ltd.
Milton Keynes UK
UKRC02n0026271017
311711UK00003B/22